MY Magic Hat Rules!

Written by Debi Novotny

Illustrated by Thea Schaeffer

This book is dedicated to my family and
friends and to those who strive to bring
literature into the life of a child.

For Scarlet and Claire,
 Enjoy the magic of reading!
  ♡ Debi Novotny

I found a magic hat one day and wore it on my **head.**

I didn't take it off
until I went to bed.

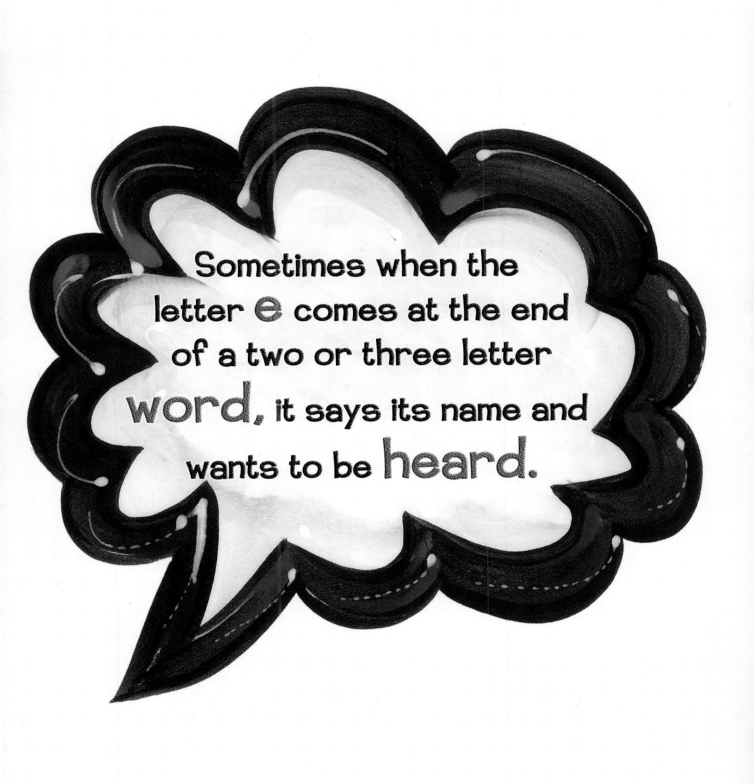

Words like   All say

he

be

she

we

me

I asked my hat for some advice.
It helped me once,
it helped me twice.

Thanks to my wonderful magic hat,
I can read words just like that.

What a big job for
such a small letter.
When I read these words,
I feel much better.

he

be

we

she

me

I found a magic
hat one day and
wore it on my
head.

I didn't take it off
until I went to bed.

Words like

ant sun

net pin

all have short vowel sounds.
It's where we begin!

I asked my hat for some advice.
It helped me once,
it helped me twice.

Thanks to my
wonderful magic hat,
I can read words
just like that.

Most words have a vowel,

reading words is what we do!

I found a magic
hat one day and
wore it on my
head.

I didn't take it off
until I went to bed.

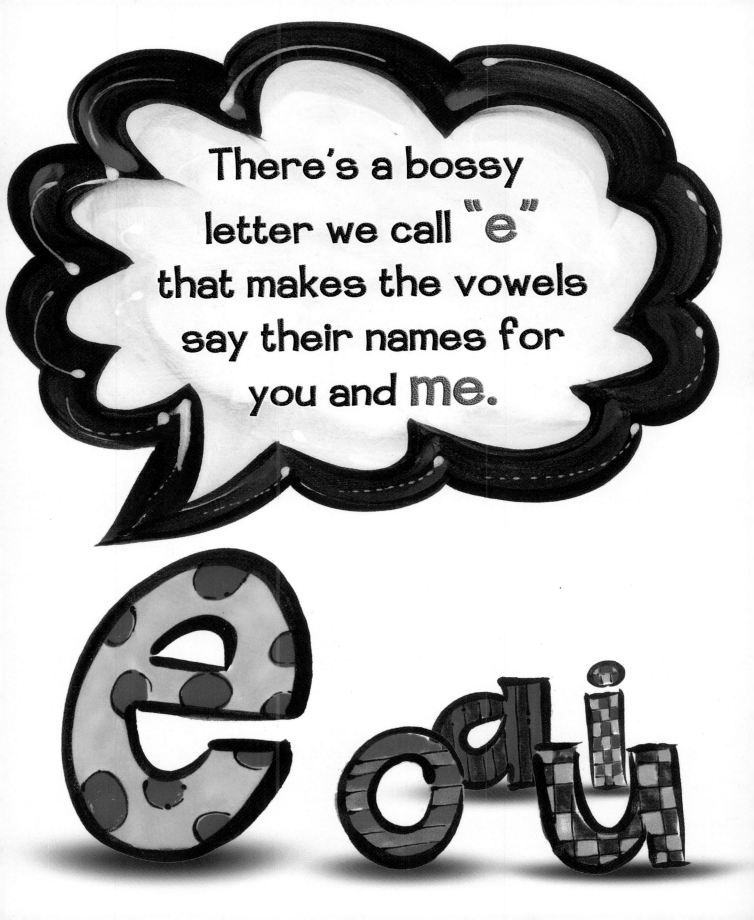

I asked my hat for some advice.
It helped me once,
it helped me twice.

Thanks to my
wonderful magic hat,
I can read words
just like that.

Now that's a rule we don't want to **forget.**

cap + e = cape
kit + e = kite
not + e = note
cut + e = cute
bit + e = bite

With my new hat,
there's nothing to **fret.**

I found a magic hat one day and wore it on my head.

I didn't take it off
until I went to bed.

 Boat says

 Seal says

 Train says

There are so many more.
This is a rule we can't ignore.

I asked my hat for some advice.
It helped me once,
it helped me twice.

Thanks to my wonderful magic hat,
I can read words just like that.

sneak

beat

peak

reach

treat

Practice reading every day, phonics rules are here to stay!

oa	ai	ea
coat	train	real
float	brain	deal
goat	gain	meal
boat	mail	meat
soap	snail	seat
goal	tail	heat
foam	pail	read
soak	paint	lead

Author Debi Novotny (left) and illustrator Thea Schaeffer (right) are both from beautiful Arizona. This duo has combined their talents to bring you a timeless book that highlights four important reading rules for beginners. It's their hope that *My Magic Hat Rules!* will reach children all over the world to help them on their journey of becoming a talented reader!